It was becoming increasingly obvious that the man who had made the tapes had made a grave error in using this electric pentacle. Whatever he had done had opened new doors in the house to places that would have been better left undisturbed. And John wasn't sure as yet how he could go about closing those doors—or if it was even possible.

He did know where he should start—back down in the basement—but the thing he'd seen in number seven had him badly spooked.

He considered seeking reinforcements—old Mr. Laws maybe—but again he heard the previous concierge's Scottish brogue, explaining the rules of the place as he carved the sigil into John's belly.

"Anything goes wrong, get off your arse and fix it. That's your job. Don't get the other folks involved. They've got enough fucking problems without worrying about yours."

John sighed, got off his arse, and went to do his job.

PENTACLE

WILLIAM MEIKLE

—1—

John stopped before the middle eight and put down the guitar. It rang mournfully, demanding more, and his sigil itched like a newly formed scab beneath his shirt. But they'd have to wait—she'd have to wait—whatever was downstairs had made a noise again, and it was past time he went to investigate.

More than that, it was his duty—he owed it to the other residents to nip things in the bud before their delicate balance was disturbed.

As he walked out into the hall, the old guitar sent out a warning ring. His sigil flared in pain, as if it had been two hours and not two years since he'd been under the knife. A truck rumbled along the Grassmarket outside and sent the foundations of the old house vibrating. The council had diverted the heavy traffic this past week, away from the workings on the tramlines in Princes Street, and down this way. The house didn't seem too happy at the idea.

Maybe that was all it is—maybe it's just the old house complaining about the traffic?

He knew better than that. Nothing in this house was ever quite what it seemed. He'd become used to that idea now, but

1

the sound that had been coming up from the basement for days was something different again, and he had a bad feeling that it wasn't anything he wanted to go near.

But what choice do I have? It comes with the job.

He slipped the hefty key chain off his belt loop and flipped through the cold iron until he found what he was looking for. It wasn't the largest key in the bunch, but it looked to be the oldest, rusted to a burnt red, and ice cold to the touch. It squealed and complained as he turned it in the lock. The house suddenly felt quiet and still, as if it had taken in a breath and was waiting to exhale.

He realized even as he pushed the door open that he hadn't been down below since his first day on the job—there had just never been any reason to venture into the musty depths.

Well, there's reason enough now.

Waves of cold, dry air came up from below. He stood at the top of the stairs, listening, not yet sure whether any repeat of the sound would make him go down, or make him turn back for the sad but familiar solace of the guitar.

All was quiet, but the house felt far from calm. He'd got used to the rhythms of the place since moving in, and knew the old house intimately. Something had it feeling antsy—something he needed to investigate before it became a definite problem.

He fumbled for the switch to his left. At first his hand met only stone and cobwebs, then he found it—a cracked plastic unit that looked to have been there since the original wiring was done in the house. He flicked the switch, half expecting to blow a fuse.

A single naked bulb flared just overhead, dimmed then steadied. It swung lazily on a fraying cord, barely lighting a steep set of stone stairs leading down; the worn steps looked like they could be even older than the house itself, certainly far

2

older than the wiring. That got him thinking about the old town and its, often bloody, history.

Is this another place where the bodies were hidden?

Edinburgh, as befitting a city of its age and history, had many stories to its name—lurid accounts of body snatching and ghosts, demonologists and witches and all kinds of goblins and bogles. And then there was the house itself. It was not the subject of any tales that John had ever been told—its secrets were, after all, more arcane than most—but it was just as fascinating, mysterious and, yes, terrifying as any of the old yarns.

He realized he was woolgathering; busy work to avoid actually going down into darkness. If he stood there long enough, one of the residents might come across him.

And then I'd have to explain what I'm doing here.

He told his legs to move, and eventually they agreed with him. He went down slowly, ready to run at the slightest provocation, listening for any sound that might give him an excuse.

After six steps, he snapped out of it.

What exactly are you afraid of, man? It can't be any worse than what's upstairs, can it?

His sigil chose that moment to tell him otherwise, sending a lancing jolt through the wound on his belly and threatening to bend him over with pain. He pushed his way through it—if there was trouble in the basement, he needed to know about it, not run from it—and followed the steps down. There were fifteen more steps before he reached bottom. He was now well below street level and the air here was colder, almost frigid. His breath steamed ahead of him, and he wished he'd taken the time to put on a heavier shirt.

The stone steps opened out onto a low-ceilinged basement that ran under the full extent of the old house. Most of the area

3

was shored up with red brick, badly pointed and cracked in places, but the far wall from where John stood was rough-hewn stone, as if it had been hacked straight out of the bedrock. The whole area was cloaked in semidarkness, lit by two more naked bulbs hanging on ancient wiring, but it looked just like it had on the day that the previous concierge had shown it to John.

White sheets covered old furniture, stacks of books had been piled up in the corners, old paintings and portraits lay stacked against the walls, and dusty mirrors reflected his pale, tense expression back at him at every turn as he crept farther into the basement, searching for the source of the noise that had disturbed him earlier. John was used to quiet—that was normal for the old building—but this felt deeper than that, almost sepulchral, and to make any sudden noise down here would feel like farting in a silent church. Nothing moved, and all John heard was the thudding of his heartbeat in his ears.

The pain from his sigil slowly eased, allowing him to relax slightly. Another truck rambled along the road outside and he felt the vibration through his soles before the silence descended completely again. And still he stood there, waiting.

If the sound had only happened once, he might have been able to pass it off as old-house noises, but he'd heard it three times now. It had definitely been a man's voice, and that wasn't a coincidence, not in this place.

"Hello?" John said, aware even as he did it that he'd laugh at himself if he saw the situation in a movie. But just like in the movies, he got an answer, of sorts.

"There are houses like this all over the world," a Scottish male voice said, casually, almost conversationally. After John's urge to run had faded, he found the source—an old personal cassette recorder under one of the white sheets, sitting beside a box of half a dozen or so tapes. He saw the cogs that drove the tape were straining, as if trying to turn, some surge from almost-

dead batteries was intermittently moving the tape along, and hence the voice.

Despite his trepidation, he'd found a rational explanation after all. And now that his fears had abated, curiosity had kicked in. The tapes all had the address of the house on their labels, along with dates, all covering the space of a month or so in the early Seventies. John knew little of the place's history beyond what the last concierge had told him, and that had only been enough to enable him to do his job. This might be a chance to delve deeper, get some sense of both the *how* and *why* of the old house.

He made his way slowly back upstairs, cradling the cassette recorder and tapes in his arms.

The cassette player, though old, looked to be in good working order. John remembered owning a similar model in his youth—listening to tinny versions of metal albums in the days when everything was analog and mainly in black and white. To today's kids it would seem as useful as an artifact from an ancient civilization, but it was a welcome burst of instant nostalgia for John.

Even more if I can get it working.

The folks upstairs were all quiet, and he'd finished his chores for the day, so he had the time, if not quite the patience, to make sure he got it done right. It took him an hour or so to clean the mechanism of dust; he had to oil the cogs and file off a thin layer of rust to get them moving. If the player had ever had a power cord, it had been long since lost, and he wasn't about to go back down to the basement to look for it. He found some batteries in the dresser that would power the machine— they'd been in the kitchen longer than John had, but they worked just fine. The old guitar rang twice, seeking company, and his sigil flared as he was finally ready to select a tape, but he ignored them both. This was something he needed to do.

Finally it was ready. The first tape was dated 25 January, 1972, and it didn't tell him anything he didn't know already.

"There are houses like this all over the world. Most people only know of them from whispered stories over campfires; tall tales told to scare the unwary. But some...those who suffer...know better. They are drawn to these places to ease their pain. If you have the will, the fortitude, you can peer into another life, where the dead are not gone, where your love might live forever.

"I first heard of this one in a bar, drowning some of my many sorrows after Meg left me. I took it for a tall tale at first—well, you would, wouldn't you—but something about it gnawed away at me. I spent long nights in pubs all over the city, asking too many questions and coming too close to getting my head kicked in.

"But I've found it—I'm here.

"The thing is, I'm not exactly sure where here is. It seems adrift from time, a capsule, entirely self-contained with its own rules and regulations—rules I must learn quickly. I have managed to glean some ideas..."

The rest of the first tape was filled with the man's speculation as to the nature of the house and how it functioned. He waffled on for a while about how the sigils worked, why there was a need for the totems, how long the houses had existed—all things John had wondered about—and with the same lack of resolution. The tape wound to an end with a click and reversed itself to play the other side, but there was nothing there except white noise and static.

The previous concierge's voice spoke in his head as he switched off the machine and removed the tape, the old Highlander's drunken brogue still easily brought to mind these two years later.

"If the shite *works,* dinnae *fuck with it."*

There was a heavy thud overhead—Mrs. Gemmell moving around in number seven probably. He waited to see if she would call out for him, but she didn't. He thought that maybe he should just take the recorder back downstairs and cover it up again, start paying attention to his real duties, but the beginning of the second tape made him sit up and take notice.

It was dated 27 January, 1972.

"Tell me how it began," the same Scottish male voice said. A woman answered. Her voice came through soft, barely more than a whisper, with a tremble to it that might have been age or sickness. John had to turn up the volume to hear her properly.

"It started with the noises in the basement."

—2—

Footsteps echoed in the hallway. The old guitar rang again as the vibrations reached it—a minor chord, so John already knew it was either the occupant of number five or number seven. He switched off the tape player and went to the door. Seven it was—Mrs. Gemmell—and from the expression on her face, she wasn't too happy about something.

"You've got to come, Mr. Philips," she said. Everyone else in the house called him John, but for some reason he couldn't fathom, the lady had never taken to him. Even now it looked like the mere act of asking him for a favor was something she found slightly repellant. And before John could answer, she was off and away back upstairs. It seemed her request was more in the nature of an order. John looked back at the tape recorder on the table.

It can wait. Duty calls.

The house felt still, almost expectant. There was a heaviness in the air he wasn't used to, and a dullness of sound, as if it was being muffled by baffles. Everything was just slightly off-kilter, and John's nerves were already on edge as he followed the woman upstairs and into her room—her sanctuary.

8

Mrs. Gemmell's room—number seven—was an homage to a certain period of British culture that John had never quite understood. Most of the furniture was bright white, curved, plastic and shiny; an afghan lay sprawled like a heavily laundered dead sheep on the floor, and a variety of lava lamps bubbled on glass-topped tables. The only thing that looked remotely comfortable was a hideous bright red leatherette sofa that dominated the wall under the windows of the small apartment. Mrs. Gemmell already sat on it, legs curled beneath her, her miniskirt hoisted up, showing lurid purple tights and an expanse of thigh John would have found unseemly in a woman thirty or forty years younger. In her right hand she held a long cigarette holder—ebony by the looks of it—and the air stank of stale tobacco and menthol. She had been crying—he saw that now—the panda rings of blue eye shadow starting to run down her cheeks. Her platinum blonde wig had skewed off slightly, giving her a lopsided look, and her lipstick—purple to match the tights—had been smeared across much of the lower half of her face. She pointed at a long, low coffee table on which sat a reel-to-reel tape recorder that seemed to be molded from lime-green plastic. John was wondering if the old woman had bought it to deliberately clash with the décor in some kind of post-modernist irony.

"It's Derek. Something's wrong with Derek." The old woman was close to tears.

He'd heard of Derek often—everybody in the building had. Mrs. Gemmell's totem was the tape player, her link to what had once been her life, her connection to her loss. Her large collection of tapes, which she played constantly to the exclusion of any other activity except smoking, were all of Derek. He spent interminable hours reciting what had always sounded to John like old hippie bollocks—long, rambling poems about love and flowers and harmony that might have been okay in sunny

9

California, but sounded misplaced in a broad Scots accent on a rainy day in Edinburgh.

"What seems to be the matter?" John said, not seeing anything immediately amiss in the room beyond Mrs. Gemmell's obvious distress.

"Something's wrong with Derek," she said again, speaking slowly and enunciating each word as if speaking to a child. "What bit of that don't you understand?"

Realizing he wasn't going to get anything more out of the woman, John went over and switched on the tape player. Derek's voice started up—something about a wizard, a dragon and a quest. But after two stanzas in, the noise started in the background. At first John took it to be a flaw in the tape, a scratch or a tear. Then the noise came again—it sounded like an animal, a dog perhaps—sniffing and snuffling, like they do when they're looking for something. As the tape played on, the noise crescendoed until it was almost drowning out the bad poetry.

"Switch it off," the woman shouted from behind him. "Just switch it off."

John did as he was told, but the sound of the snuffling seemed to continue to echo round the room long after the reels stopped spinning.

"Something's wrong with Derek," the woman whispered through fresh tears. "Fix it. That's your job, isn't it? Just get it fixed."

As John left the room, the woman scratched at her stomach under her blouse, as if her sigil, which must have been decades old and long healed, was giving her pain.

The delicate balance of the house had been disturbed. It was evident in the air, underfoot, and even in the way light and shade played on the landing as he walked out of number seven. Something was different, and had been since he'd noticed the sounds in the basement. The television was on, was always on, in number five; *Coronation Street* was playing—a Seventies' episode if John remembered right. He heard the old man talk to the set, conversing with someone from another time, another place. At least Mr. Laws hadn't been affected yet. And all seemed quiet and normal both across the hall and on the upper landing.

Maybe it's only Mrs. Gemmell having problems?

But the house didn't work that way—he'd been here long enough to know that much. The voice from the second tape gave him a clue as to where to begin.

It started with the noises in the basement.

He went straight down to his room beside the main doorway—the concierge's apartment—his place, his duty. The guitar rang as he entered, but his old friend sounded dull and lifeless, all magic leeched out of her.

He picked her up, caressed her gently. They'd been together too long for him to be able to ignore her pain. He stroked a D minor, then again, and kept playing until she started to seem more like her old self.

He sang, an old favorite, one that she'd always liked.

As fair art thou, my bonnie lass,
So deep in love am I,
And I will love thee still, my dear,
Till a' the seas gang dry.

The old guitar's voice wasn't quite in tune with him. It sounded harsh, almost grating, and for the first time in two years, he got no joy out of it. The next verse made it worse still.

Till a' the seas gang dry, my dear,
And the rocks melt wi' the sun,
And I will love thee still, my dear,

11

While the sands o' life shall run.

At this point he usually heard Lizzie's voice—high, soft, and sweet—accompanying him as she had done so often for so many years in bars and clubs across the country. But this time there was no singing, just a far-off wail of piteous sobbing. He'd heard that before—before he took his job in the house. He didn't like it any better this time around.

"Lizzie?"

He got no answer, and when he put the guitar down, it hit the floor with a dull thud, all pretense at musicality erased from it. His sigil throbbed with a deep ache that seemed to reach down into his bones.

Something was definitely wrong with the house.

Fix it. That's your job, isn't it? Just get it fixed.

The trouble was he wasn't sure where to start. He switched on the cassette player and listened to the second tape.

> *"It started three weeks ago, just after the New Year, with the noises in the basement,"* **the old woman's voice whispered.** *"At first it was groaning and rumbling, and we thought it was the old place settling, maybe getting disturbed by the road workings up on the Castle Esplanade. But they began coming at night, when the Auld Lady was sleeping.*
>
> *"Jimmy Fallon in number seven noticed it first, in the painting above his fireplace.*
>
> *"'There's too many shadows,' he said one morning as he joined me for a coffee and a smoke. 'Too much darkness—and she's not there.'*

"It wasn't long before the rest of us took notice. Shadows where there shouldn't be shadows, weeping where there should be laughing, and that weird snuffling sound every which way you turn—our sigils hurt, our totems failed, and the house showed us the full extent of our misery. There has been talk of leaving—but where would we go? We're here because we have to be here—but there's something broken—the house broke."

The cultured male voice spoke again.

"And how did you fix it?"

"We didn't," the woman replied, a sob in her voice. *"It's still going on. Help us. You seem to know something about this stuff. You have to help us."*

There was nothing else on the second tape but white noise and hiss. When John started hearing sniffing amid the random sounds, he switched the machine off, but it seemed that the sounds continued, far-off and distant, long after the tape stopped running.

—3—

John spent a sleepless night, his mind racing with the implications of both his experiences of the night before, and what he'd heard on the tape. It all boiled down to one thing.

The house can be broken. Nobody told me that was possible.

He lay staring at the ceiling, remembering the speech he'd got when he turned up on the doorstep. He'd just been wandering, aimless and lost like he had been since Lizzie passed. He'd played a gig in a bar on the Royal Mile the night before and now, in the early dawn, he found himself in the Grassmarket. Something about the house had drawn him, and before he knew it, he'd knocked on the door, trying to formulate an excuse before someone opened it and told him to bugger off.

Instead, he got a strong handshake, and the offer of a coffee, over which, among other things, he was told that he'd been expected.

"There are houses like this all over the world," the old concierge had said as they finished the coffee, then shared the best part of a bottle of good Scotch. As he remembered, John realized it was almost exactly the same words he'd heard earlier on the tape.

I wonder if everybody gets the same speech?

"Most people only know of them from whispered stories over campfires; tall tales told to scare the unwary. But some of us, those who suffer…some of us know better. We are drawn to the places, the loci if you like, where what ails us can be eased. Yes, dead is dead, as it was and always will be. But there are other worlds than these, other possibilities. And if we have the will, the fortitude, we can peer into another life, where the dead are not gone, where we can see that they thrive and go on. And as we watch and listen, we can, sometimes, gain enough peace for ourselves that we too can thrive, and go on."

The old man had downed a glass of liquor that would have floored John if he'd tried it. At the same time, he scratched idly at his belly, as if picking at an old scar.

"You will want to know more than why," he had continued. "You will want to know how. I cannot tell you that. None of us has ever known, only that the house is important, and that a sigil and a totem are needed to make it work."

"What do you mean, work?" John had asked.

"Ah," the old man replied. "That's the easy bit. I think I know already what your totem is—you carry it plainly enough. Would you give me a tune?"

It had been the least he could do after the old man's hospitality. He'd taken out the guitar and started up—not quite his favorite song, but certainly Lizzie's.

My love is like a red, red rose,
That's newly sprung in June.
My love is like the melody,
That's sweetly played in tune.

He had to stop before he reached the end of the first verse, for there was clearly someone singing along with him—and it wasn't the old man—it was Lizzie—her clear high alto unmistakable as it covered for his gruff bass notes.

"Is this some kind of trick?" he'd asked, and the old man had just smiled.

"I've got an idea for you, if you're interested." he'd said.

John's sigil flared in hot pain as he remembered the old man cutting the red rose into his belly—none too carefully. The Scotch had helped, but even so, he probably wouldn't ever forget that hour, with the cold knife at his skin, the old man swearing like a dockhand and the sweat pouring off him. As he cut, the old man talked—much of it sounded like nonsense at the time and only made sense to John much later—laying down the rules of the house, the terms of John's entry to the place.

A week later the old man was dead and John, along with his guitar, moved into room one—the house had a new concierge, and John was reacquainted with an old love. He gave up gigging and moved what little he owned into the small apartment. By day he managed the running of the place—in truth there wasn't much to it—and by night he played, while Lizzie sang with him.

And so it had gone, each day much like the last.

Until now.

How do I fix something if I don't really know how it works?

He was still pondering that question when thin sunlight streaming through the curtains heralded the morning of another day.

He didn't pull the curtains back. There was no need—there was never any view. The windows were almost opaque—a flat gray that allowed no sight of the world outside beyond occasional shifting shadows. Besides, John wasn't always sure the world was there outside for much of the time. He'd ventured up onto the roof once—just once—and there he'd met the same flat gray, everywhere, like an all-encompassing mist.

16

He had come to believe the house mostly existed elsewhere and elsewhen, allowing egress for occupants when they needed to go out for food and drink, which wasn't often. John stocked his own larder for weeks at a time in one trip, and he knew most of the others did the same.

None of which was helping him solve his current problem.

He made a coffee, the guitar stayed quiet, and put the third tape, dated 30 January, 1972, into the cassette player.

"I will make a start," the cultured man's voice said. *"The electric pentacle I found downstairs still works, although I had to purchase a new battery to power the valves, and the wiring may well be on its last legs. I am not entirely sure what the thing does, but the mere fact of finding it here, in this place, tells me it is of great import, and may well be the source of what ails this place. In any case, it is too interesting to ignore.*

"I have the original notes that were stored alongside it here with me, and the incantations are simple enough, but they are lengthy, and I am afraid this might take some time.

"Even the preparations were rather extensive, but thankfully it is detailed fully in the notebook. I did as it told me, and started by drawing a circle of chalk, taking care never to smudge the line as I navigated my way around the space in the basement. Beyond this, I rubbed a broken garlic clove in a second circle around the first.

"When this was done, I took a small jar of water that had been blessed by a priest and went

17

round the circle again just inside the line of chalk, leaving a wet trail that dried quickly behind me. Within the inner circle I made my pentacle using the signs of the Saaamaaa Ritual as detailed in the notes, and joined each sign most carefully to the edges of the lines I had already made.

"In the points of the pentacle I placed five portions of bread wrapped in linen, and in the valleys five phials of the holy water. Now I had my first protective barrier and with this first stage complete, the basement—indeed the whole house—already felt more secure, as if a great calmness had fallen over the property.

"I set the valves and cabling to overlay the drawn pentagram upon the floor. When I connected the battery, an azure glare shone out, washing the whole basement in waves of color. It is strangely hypnotic and soothing.

"That was all done several minutes ago, and I am now ready to proceed. The next part requires that I stand inside the circle I have drawn. I shall leave the recorder running—at the very least it shall provide a record of what has happened, and perhaps, just perhaps, I will manage to capture on tape an indication of what ails this place."

The tape hissed for several seconds then a chant rose up. John recognized it as Gaelic, although he did not understand the words.

"Ri linn dioladh na beatha, Ri linn bruchdadh na falluis, Ri linn iobar na creadha, Ri linn dortadh na fala."

18

The tape went quiet again, exuding only the most whispered of hisses. Something sniffed and snuffled—a sound too similar to what John had heard in number seven earlier for it to be a coincidence. Then, as if someone had turned the volume up full, the small room exploded with noise. A high, wild scream seemed to pour out of the cassette player, so loud, so grating that John leaned forward and shut it off to avoid having to hear it any longer.

He thought the screaming echoed in his head, for he could still hear it, faint as if far-off. It took him several seconds to realize the noise was coming from upstairs, directly over his head.

He bounded up the staircase three steps at a time. By the time he was halfway up, he knew exactly where the sound originated—Mrs. Gemmell was screaming as if she was being tortured.

Doors opened as John passed, but none of the other residents came out to help him, and he was still alone as he reached the door to number seven. He didn't slow; he put his shoulder into it and burst inside.

Mrs. Gemmell lay, legs akimbo, on the white sheepskin rug—a rug that was splattered in flecks of red. Blood dripped from the woman's nose but she didn't seem to notice. She didn't even look round when John entered. Her whole attention was on the long coffee table and the tape deck.

The reel-to-reel player, and the air all around and above it, swirled in ink-black shadows that seethed and roiled in impossible vortices and whorls. The machine was playing, and the noise was all too familiar—sniffing and snuffling, as if a huge beast was lurking in the shadows, searching for something. And now there was something else, only the faintest of odors, but it reminded John far too much of the time he'd found a dead crow behind a closed-off fireplace.

Without thinking, John rushed forward and upended the table and tape player, smashing both to the floor in a tangled mess of plastic, glass and spiraling cascades of tape running off the spools. The snuffling stopped. The black swirling shadows fell apart and vanished, leaving John standing in a suddenly too-quiet, too-still room, with Mrs. Gemmell staring, first at the ruined tape player, then to John, then back to the mess on the floor.

"What have you done?" she whispered.

Then she burst into tears.

—4—

It took most of the morning to calm down Mrs. Gemmell, and even then it was more due to copious amounts of gin than anything John could have said or done. He left her sleeping on the couch by the windows and made his way out into the hallway. A party of householders stood silently waiting for him on the landing. It looked like Mr. Laws had been nominated as spokesman, although the old man didn't seem too happy about it. He put a hand on John's arm, his grip surprisingly strong, belying his age.

"See here, John, this just won't do. How am I supposed to watch the street with this racket going on? It won't do at all. We can't be doing with fuss and nonsense—you know that."

John nodded.

"Aye, I know. Trust me, I'm working on something. Just go back to your rooms and let me get on with it. Please?"

Their eyes were filled with worry—and fear—both of which John felt rising inside himself. At first he thought they might argue further, but Mrs. Gemmell had stopped sobbing, for now at least, and once again the house was falling quiet around them. They drifted off to their respective rooms. Old Mr. Laws waited until everyone had gone, and leaned in close to whisper to John, as if afraid to be overheard.

"Stop this thing, son," he said. "Stop it before it comes through. You don't want it to come through."

And with that cryptic remark, the old man turned and went to his own room, leaving John alone at the top of the stairs.

He noticed again that something was off—the old house made him feel on edge again, as twitchy as he'd once been before he ever discovered the place. He wanted—needed—a drink and a smoke, and that was never a good sign. The stairs creaked underfoot as he descended, and something fluttered like a moth against a window, high up in the rafters, although when he looked up, he saw nothing but hanging motes of dust dancing in watery sunlight. Even as he watched, the light seemed to fade as shadows gathered and swirled, reminding him all too forcibly of the shifting blackness he'd seen right before he'd destroyed Mrs. Gemmell's tape player.

If something starts snuffling, I'm out of here.

He headed for his room as fast as he could without giving the impression of actually running away.

Even the normally relaxing feel of the guitar in his arms didn't soothe him. The instrument didn't sing, didn't laugh or cry, just lay, dead wood against his chest. He strummed a few chords that were swallowed and eaten by the leaden atmosphere. He tried to sing.

Till a' the seas gang dry, my dear,
And the rocks melt wi' the sun,
And I will love thee still, my dear,
While the sands o' life shall run.

The walls swallowed his song and gave him nothing back. Lizzie stayed quiet and the guitar didn't ring when he put it back on its stand in the corner.

Yep. Something is definitely off.

The cassette player still sat on the table, with the third tape in it, but John remembered that last scream only too well and wasn't about to listen to it again. He switched tapes and put in number four, then made himself a fresh pot of coffee before settling down to listen, ready to switch off at the first sign of any more trouble.

The tape was dated 6 February, 1972.

"It has been a week now, and I am still shaken to my core," the soft, now recognizable, voice started. He did not sound quite so cultured now—there was an edge to his tone, something that almost sounded like fear.

"The notes I found with the pentacle warned me there might be some danger, but, by God I never expected... Wait, let me back up and explain.

"If you have been listening to these tapes, you will have heard the scream. Yes, that was me, at least I'm pretty sure it was me, although things got mighty strange toward the end there.

"As soon as I stood inside the pentagram, I knew I had made a mistake. I wasn't ready—I might never be ready—but I made a promise and I had to try. The house is worth it, even if I have to sacrifice my sanity.

"I felt tingly—I can't really describe it any better than that—as if a mild current was flowing over my body. That and a feeling of

lightheadedness, similar to having drunk too much Scotch, but without any associated dizziness. I have never taken any of the so-called mind-expanding drugs, but I have a feeling what I experienced within that electric pentacle may well have been of a similar nature to some of the reported effects of LSD.

"My vision blurred until all I could see was the swirling dance of color from the pentacle valves. Something took hold of my senses, and my mind roamed elsewhere, until after a time my vision seemed to clear.

"I was in a high place, soaring like an eagle above a barren plain under a purple sky. It seemed I spent hours there in the air, drifting slowly toward an unseen destination, but I felt no worry, no fear. It was not like being in a dream at all, I can tell you that. Everything seemed vibrant and alive. I felt hot wind on my face, heard it rush in my ears, and I could taste the air, acrid and bitter, like cheap tobacco. I was so enamored by the sense of freedom I felt that I failed to notice I was hovering above a huge black pyramid until I was almost on top of it. The structure was carved from a single piece of stone, like jet but somehow darker still, with a sheen to it that made it shimmer, like far-off buildings on a hot summer's day.

"I tried to back away, but a compulsion held me, and drew me down ever closer. I resolved to go along, believing I might acquire knowledge that would help me, help the people in the house.

"At that very moment, deep down inside the pyramid, something stirred, something knew I was there, something waiting for me. It was time for me to seize some control of the situation. I looked down at the dark hole at the top of the structure and willed myself into its dark maw. I was almost surprised when it worked and I descended ever more rapidly. Shortly I was inside the structure itself, and falling through darkness.

"Fortunately, the farther down I went, the more my eyes adjusted, until soon I was able to ascertain the nature of the place.

"Everything was bathed in a thin green dancing light and the pyramid seemed to be a massive empty shell, sepulchral, like a huge cathedral. I was still high above the floor of the building but already I saw things moving below. The floor was covered in a viscous green fluid, bubbling and frothing, throwing high spouts upward only for them to fall back with a splash to the lake of slime. Thicker globules seemed to swim through the fluid and as I inched closer they gained mass, swelling into familiar shapes—a torso, two legs, two arms, and a head, too round, but almost human...apart from the flat snouts that gave the faces an almost pig-like appearance.

"Ten of them grew from the slime and stood, stock-still.

"As one, they lifted their heads and stared straight at the point where I hung.

"*They sniffed the air, as if sensing my presence.*

"*I tried to speak the words of the dismissal spell, but if I had a throat and vocal cords in that place, they did not seem to be functioning. I drifted ever lower and the snouts rose in the air, snuffling in almost frantic anticipation.*

"*I might be still be there, snuffling alongside them, had I not finally managed to bring the exorcism spell to the front of my mind.*

"*I shouted.*

"*Ri linn dioladh na beatha, Ri linn bruchdadh na falluis, Ri linn iobar na creadha, Ri linn dortadh na fala.*

"*I started to rise up out of the pyramid, slowly at first, then faster and faster, 'til I was being propelled at dizzying speeds through jet-black space, a snell wind whistling in my ears. Faster and faster I flew, all rational thought being blasted from my mind by the sheer speed of flight and the immensity of the space through which I traveled.*

"*Weeks passed, and still I flew, through clouds of gas that engulfed whole systems of stars. I traveled through blackness so empty and devoid of anything that it hurt my soul to even consider it, and passed worlds that had once teemed with life but were now as dead and dust-ridden as the most ancient of ruins. My brain could not encompass this journey, could not process it.*

"*Finally, after an age, I woke with a jolt as if I had been rudely thrust back into my body,*

26

and felt at first as if I had been fitted inside a badly tailored meat-suit. I was back in the pentacle, encased in a swirling vortex of color, blues and greens and gold shifting so fast I felt nauseated and ready to give myself over to a dead faint.

"I quickly came back to equilibrium when I heard a noise—a loud snuffle. At first I believed it to be a remnant of that strange vision, but then it came again, louder this time, more insistent.

"It sounded like it came from inside the basement.

"The colors of the pentacle thinned and parted, enough for me to see quite clearly that a shadow shifted in the corner.

"It snuffled again.

"And that's when I screamed."

John stopped the tape to fetch a fresh cup of coffee from the pot. He was starting to get a feel for what was going on—the man who made the tapes had arrived in the house and tried to help with whatever seemed to be happening. But without a sigil or a token, he simply blundered about in the dark.

And it looked like he'd blundered upon what he called the pentagram—what John guessed, given it had been found in the basement—a long-discarded token that had belonged to another resident.

That was another rule of the house, another one John always heard in the heavy Scottish accent of the previous concierge.

"You dinna *fuck with anybody's else's stuff. The house* disnae *like it."*

27

That much was now self-evident. John still didn't know how to fix the problem, but at least he was coming to understand the nature of it. He took a deep slug of coffee, leaned forward, and started up the cassette recorder again, straight from where he'd left off.

"The next thing I remember I was up in the hall by the front door, breathing heavily. I stood there for a long time, just listening, but there was no repeat of the snuffling.

"I have spent the best part of this week trying to calm my nerves, for I was frightened, and it was only the concierge that stopped me from packing my bag and fleeing. He said all I needed was time—that the house had recognized me, and my task here was a worthy one.

"In the immediate aftermath of my time in the pentacle, I was not so sure of his assessment, but now that I have some distance and time from it, I can look back at it, if not quite dispassionately, at least with some degree of curiosity. It may well be some days yet before I can bring myself to return to the basement, though. Besides, there are other more pressing matters that require my attention right now, particularly in number seven.

"Jimmy Fallon called me up this morning— something about the mirror, he said. 'There's darkness in it that shouldn't be there.'

"As soon as I saw what he meant, I recognized it immediately—a black shadow—a pyramid in the far distance. Even as I looked at it, gazing into the impossibly far depths in the

*mirror, I knew this was somehow my fault—my
ritual in the basement had done far more harm
than good.*

*"And whatever was happening was
spreading, fast. Old Jimmy heard it first, I
think—he put a hand on my shoulder and
clenched it, tight enough to cause me pain.*

"'Did you hear that?'

*"I didn't the first time, but I did the second,
and the third.*

*"Something sat, hidden in the dark corner by
the fireplace—something large—something that
snuffled."*

John switched off the tape and rose from the table, suddenly
driven by a need to check on Mrs. Gemmell in number seven.
The old guitar rang as he passed it, a minor seventh that said
stay. His sigil flared in fresh pain as if to reinforce the message,
but duty was duty, and he was already guilty enough at having
wrecked the woman's totem. He took the stairs three at a time
again, and he was out of breath by the time he reached the
landing outside her room.

The only sound was the thudding of his heartbeat in his
ears—there wasn't even a snatch of *Coronation Street* dialogue
to disturb the blanket of quiet that had fallen over the house.
John took a few moments to compose himself before knocking
softly on the door.

"Mrs. Gemmell? It's John. Can I come in?"

No answer.

He stepped closer to the door.

Something inside snuffled softly. It might have been Mrs.
Gemmell crying, but John didn't think so. He stood still, but the

29

noise wasn't repeated. He put his hand on the door handle, just as it turned from the other side.

He stopped and held his breath. The brass handle went cold in his palm, and when he did finally breathe, mist formed in the air ahead of him.

"Mrs. Gemmell?"

A snuffling sound in reply.

"I'm coming in," he shouted, with more bravado than he felt, and turned the handle. The door swung open, revealing a dim room beyond. Although it was still afternoon, the curtains were drawn over all the windows, and there were no lights on. John could just make out the remains of the tape deck strewn on the floor, but the rest of the room was lost in soft, swirling shadows.

"Mrs. Gemmell?" he said, softly, dismayed that he hadn't managed to keep a tremor out of his voice.

A groan in reply.

He'd left her lying drunk on the couch, and that's where the latest sound had come from. He picked his way across the floor, headed in that direction. As soon as he was fully into the room, the door shut behind him, swinging closed with a dull thud that prompted another answering groan from across the room. This time he wasn't entirely sure it had come from a human throat.

Only duty kept him moving.

"Enough of the silly buggers, Mrs. Gemmell," he said. "Just speak up—let me know you're okay."

He banged his shin against a piece of furniture, cursed under his breath—a snuffle and a sniff in reply. And now he smelled it—something thick and cloying, animalistic and completely out of place in the old lady's living room. It certainly wasn't perfume.

He took two more steps, pretty sure he had reached the couch, leaned over and drew back the nearest curtain, letting thin, diffuse light into the room. A figure lay beneath him, swaddled in a thick comforter.

"Mrs. Gemmell?"

He bent and pulled back the material. A face turned to stare at him. At one time it might even have been Mrs. Gemmell, but now the features had been flattened and coarsened, the nose squat, almost snout-like, with thick, coarse hairs sprouting from huge flaring nostrils. She snuffled, as if smelling for him. Her eyes—deep and dark, like tiny pools of oil—struggled for focus, and she moved slowly, as if in great pain. John backed away as she started to shuck off the comforter, attempting to sit up.

He tripped, almost falling as he stumbled over the remains of the tape deck in his haste to retreat.

She snuffled again, and moaned. The comforter fell away, and John got a good look—a far-too-good look—at her. She was naked—pink and covered in course, stubby hair, her body grotesquely swollen—but not so much that he didn't see the twin rows of nipples, three on either side, that ran down her torso. He also saw why she had so much trouble divesting herself of the comforter—her hands had become little more than cloven stumps on the end of thick, fleshy arms. The smell, more like a stench, grew stronger, thick, musky and almost chewable.

John backed off farther, up against the door. The thing on the couch groaned and snuffled again, dragged the curtain back into place to shut out the lights, then drew itself laboriously back under the comforter. John had a bad moment when he couldn't find the door handle, then another when he thought it wasn't going to open when he pulled, but seconds later he was back out on the landing, breathing too heavily and wondering whether he had gone completely insane.

—5—

He stood outside the door long enough to ensure that nothing was going to attempt to come out after him. It took all of his nerve to put an ear against the wood and listen. There was no noise from inside at all, but in his mind he heard it, over and over again, an animal snuffle. That, even more than the sight and smell of the thing, had him rattled.

Before he went back downstairs, he unhooked his key chain and locked the door. If Mrs. Gemmell wanted out, she only had to say so, otherwise whatever was in that room was going to stay there—at least until he had a good idea what he was dealing with, and how to fix it. He went slowly back down to his own room, listening at every step for any movement from number seven, but once again the whole house had fallen silent around him. But all was not well—his sigil flared, fresh pain at his belly, and when he entered the room, the old guitar moaned dully. He ignored it and eschewed more coffee for something a bit stronger. The Scotch bottle had sat in the back of the cupboard for months, but now seemed like a good time to give it an airing. He poured himself a generous measure and, more from a need to have some noise to fill the silence than from any great desire to hear more, switched on the cassette player. It continued straight from where it had left off.

"I persuaded Mr. Fallon that discretion was the better part of valor and we left the room. I believe the old man has taken himself off to the nearest bar for a stiffener. I must admit I was close to joining him, but someone has to catalog this matter, and I'm afraid it will have to be me.

"I returned to my perusal of the notes I found with the electric pentacle. The writer, whose name I have not been able to ascertain, seems to have been a great believer in the occult, and has obviously delved deeply into arcane mysteries. Unfortunately much of his writing is impenetrable guff of the highest order. I did, however, find mention of the pyramid. Let me read the section.

"'It began with a dream.

"'I have a vision of a deep-purple sky, with dark stems rising, casting shadows from a moon too large for the sky, a red moon that rises above jagged hills. Things move among the stems, low-slung, insect-like farmers, tending to the growth.

"'And it is not just on the ground where things scurry. Something crosses the face of the moon—a thin body, propelled by gossamer wings, hovering like a vast dragonfly above the plain below.

"'I am sucked downward toward a dark edifice on the plain, a pyramidal structure enormous in scale, black as coal and swarming with drones. It has a hole in the top, a tunnel

leading down into its bowels and I know I do not want to see what is inside. I swirl down, gaining speed, spinning dizzily, accelerating toward where something waits—something that wants a closer look at me.

"'I try to scream, but nothing comes, like being caught in a nightmare and from which you can't wake yourself. I pass the mouth of the hole in the pyramid and tumble deeper into blackness. It sucks ever more eagerly at me...

"'I woke, sitting bolt upright in bed, drenched in a cold sweat with fear pounding through me.'"

The cultured voice continued.

"As you can hear, the writer of these notes has clearly had a similar experience to my own. There are also several veiled references to what he calls 'swine things'—denizens of the pyramid that can only be the source of the snuffling in the here and now. The writer appears to put great stock in the efficacy of the electric pentacle and uses it in his fight against Outer Darkness. Here's another passage from his notes.

"'I took the time to attach the colored valves of the electric pentacle to the battery, switched it on, and went to join the others in the circle. The dancing glow from the valves lit the room in a wash of color as they warmed, then flared blue in unison with a loud snuffle from outside.

"'A movement, just discernible, could be seen beyond the boarded window. Another snuffle sounded, but no closer than the last. They were

being more cautious tonight, perhaps due to my new defenses.

"'The green valve on the pentacle flared and pulsed in a definite rhythm, almost one flash per second, and getting faster all the time. The effect was mesmerizing, almost hypnotic. And whatever was outside took up the same beat, pounding against the windows in time. Any remaining glass beyond the boards broke and fell away. From my position at the fireplace I saw the boards buckle as a heavy weight pressed against them, again and again. The nails I had so assiduously pounded into place squealed and complained, but they held—for now.'

"As you can see, the pentacle seems to have been efficacious against the snuffling sounds in the past. It may be that I myself will be able to use the same device to clear the problem that ails this house. But more research is needed before I can make any attempt in that direction.

"And it will involve further descents into the basement.

"I am not altogether sure I have the nerve for it."

The tape hissed and ran out. It seemed that was the end of tape four, and once again John tried the reverse side, only to find more white noise and static. As he ejected the tape from the player, he was thinking again of the old concierge's admonishment against messing with other residents' totems. It was becoming increasingly obvious that the man who had made the tapes had made a grave error in using this electric pentacle. Whatever he had done had opened new doors in the house to places that would have been better left undisturbed.

And John wasn't sure as yet how he could go about closing those doors — or if it was even possible.

He did know where he should start — back down in the basement — but the thing he'd seen in number seven had him badly spooked. He considered seeking reinforcements — old Mr. Laws, maybe — but again he heard the previous concierge's Scottish brogue, explaining the rules of the place as he carved the sigil into John's belly.

"Anything goes wrong, get off your arse and fix it. That's your job. Don't get the other folks involved. They've got enough fucking problems without worrying about yours."

John sighed, got off his arse, and went to do his job.

The basement was as dark and quiet as it had been on his previous visit. But it felt somehow less empty, as if something lurked unseen, keeping to the edges of the shadows, out of sight.

John wasted as little time as possible in a search of the area, lifting up the white sheets to see what had been hidden. He found old pianos, radio sets, more portraits, more mirrors, and a wide variety of porcelain ornaments — but no pentacle. He did find where it had been used — the faded circle with an interior pentagram was still partly visible in an otherwise cleared patch of floor.

The darkness in the corners shifted, and the faintest hint of a musky odor wafted in the air — the same he had smelled so recently in number seven. He started to back off, more than ready to admit defeat, when his foot collided with a box underneath a dresser. He bent and looked; the first thing he saw was a pale-blue crystal valve and some badly frayed vintage electrical wiring. He didn't have time to look any closer. The shadow in the corner thickened, the smell grew stronger, tickling in his throat and nose, and something snuffled.

John picked up the box from under the dresser and, staggering slightly under the weight, rushed back up to the main hallway. He slammed the basement door shut behind him.

He couldn't know there was something, just on the other side of that door, something pink and hairy and snuffling and foul—he couldn't know. But he did. And nothing on earth was about to persuade him to go back down into that darkness anytime soon.

He took his discovery to his room and left it on the table beside the cassette player while he poured himself another Scotch.

—6—

John waited until he felt calm again before investigating the contents of the box. His old guitar rang mournfully, and his sigil sent him a burst of warning heat as he lifted the valves and wiring out of the container, but he ignored them both.

I already know there's trouble here. I need to know how much.

The box contained a dozen of the valves—ovoid crystals in a variety of colors. A smaller wooden box was tucked in a corner, containing some phials—holy water, at a guess—some chalk and several dried-up pieces of garlic.

There was also a leather-bound notebook underneath the holy water. The pages, like the leather covering, felt brittle, the writing faded in places, but legible. He put it to one side as he examined the valves carefully. They all seemed rather fragile, but he was surprised to discover they were all fully intact. The same thing could not be said for the wiring—it looked like it must have been nearly a century old, and the thin copper beneath the wrapped fibrous exterior of the cables was green and corroded in many places. Two terminals, obviously meant for attachment to a battery or generator, were in an even worse state, crumbling to rust under his touch. If he wanted to use the equipment, he would have to rewire the whole thing.

But it was at least something he could do, something to focus his mind on. Over the course of the next few hours, he cannibalized a variety of guitar leads, an old ten-watt practice amp, and several jack plugs. Then he started putting the electric pentacle back together. It was painstaking work, but absorbing. Once he got the knack of connecting the old valves, it became more about putting in the time than requiring much actual concentration.

He loaded tape five in the cassette player and set it running while he worked.

"Fallon has left the house for the weekend while I try to cleanse number seven of whatever has taken residence there. The concierge thinks I need a sigil—or rather, he has insisted on it, so I have had a small owl done on my left pectoral. Becky liked owls—we had her buried with a stuffed one. Rather than get cut, I went to a tattoo parlor off Haymarket. The blasted thing itches like crazy now, but in a way I am glad of it, for it serves to remind me of my purpose.

"The pyramid is clearer now in the mirror— more solid, more defined. Likewise, the snuffling thing in the corner, although it has not moved from the position, has become noisier, and appears to be taking a definite form. In a certain light I can see a pinkish snout—and tusks, two long, curved points that seem to catch the light and almost shine. Then there's the smell—a terrible stench, like rotting fish, but even that description does not begin to describe the foulness that assaults you upon entering the room.

"The concierge has advised merely closing the door and forgetting about it. He says the house has ways of its own to deal with intrusions such as these. But I owe Fallon more than that—I owe him my best shot at fixing what I have broken.

"I have tried to persuade the concierge that I should be utilizing the electric pentacle, but he has drawn the line at that, insisting I leave the device in the basement. Likewise, I am forbidden from even perusing the notebook, despite the fact that there must be more gems of arcane wisdom lurking within its pages.

"It seems I am on my own, but at least I now have the sigil.

"That, and my heart, will have to be enough."

Once again John was disturbed by sounds from upstairs. He switched off the tape and put down the valve he was working on—the last one. His sigil almost doubled him over with a flash of hot pain, and the guitar rang out loud and angry as he stood.

Something thudded overhead; then again—a heavy pounding that sent the light fitting swinging.

Number seven. Why did it have to be number seven?

People came out onto the landing as he went upstairs. Old Mr. Laws looked particularly pale, wide-eyed and terrified out of his wits. John tried to be calm for them.

"Just go back inside," he said. "Mrs. Gemmell's having a bad night, that's all."

Somebody guffawed loudly at that, but to John's surprise they all did as they were told, even when something hit the door of number seven with a crash that shook the whole house.

"Mrs. Gemmell?" he said, stepping toward the door. "It's John. Is everything okay?"

He tried not to think of the pink porcine thing he'd seen trying to emerge from the comforter's folds, and concentrated on a mental image of the woman herself as she'd been before all this nonsense started. He put a hand on the doorknob. Everything went quiet, but once again John knew there was something on the other side, listening.

What is it waiting for?

He tried the door. It was still locked, and solid enough to withstand any amount of pounding.

Stronger than my nerves anyway.

"I'm going to fix this, Mrs. Gemmell. I promise," he said.

He only got a snuffle as an answer—and the faintest musky animal odor in his nostrils as he turned to go downstairs. There was no repeat of the pounding—the only sound accompanying his descent was the theme tune of *Coronation Street* echoing faintly from Mr. Laws's room.

The old guitar sang to welcome him home, but it still sounded dull and lifeless. He wasn't going to get any comfort from that quarter until he'd got this sorted.

Rather than dive into a bottle, he went back to work on the pentacle. He was on the last lap now—the valves were all wired up, and all that was left to do was make a clean pair of terminals and attach them to a power source.

While he was doing that, he switched the cassette tape on. There was a short pause, hissing white noise, then the cultured man's voice took up his story again.

"The sigil is working—or at least, it is doing something. When I played back what I recorded

41

earlier, I'm sure I heard her—Becky—faint and far off, but that giggle is unmistakable. The concierge says I'm not to push it. If the house wants me, it will take me in. I tried to tell him that I only came to study the place, and stayed because I made the mistake with the pentacle and needed to fix it. He just looked at me with his big, sad eyes.

"'If the shit works, don't fuck with it,' he said in his broad Glasgow accent.

"But I'm afraid I'm going to have to. I've been up in number seven again. The thing there is almost fully through to our side now, snuffling and scraping and banging on the door when nobody is around. The pyramid is closer, too—the mirror is full of shifting shadow and light, black and gold and purple all at once in an oily iridescence that hurts the eyes to look at.

"The notebook mentioned one last ritual to end all rituals—a thing that can only be uttered once and in the time of utmost need. Given the way the beast in number seven is developing, I would say this qualifies. I have not told the concierge, but I transcribed the chant before he had me return the book to the basement. I have no idea whether my pronunciation will get the job done—but I have to try, not just for myself, but for the other poor folks here—and for my Becky. If I am to hear her again, I have to try.

"I will do it tonight."

The tape hissed and ran out. John tried the other side, but it had only white noise, although once he thought he heard a child giggle, far away, like someone shouting in the wind.

—7—

It was time to try the apparatus.

He laid the valves in a row across the floor, and hooked up the terminals to an old car battery he'd found in the shed out back. He didn't expect much, so was taken aback when the room filled with washes of color. The valves pulsed, blue and green and red and yellow—a slow, hypnotic dance.

The guitar vibrated and hummed in time, so insistent that John couldn't help but lift it into his arms. He strummed a chord—a minor seventh. The room flared in an azure blue that brought instant memories of summer days on hot beaches.

He experimented. Major chord progressions brought greens and ochre that spoke of walks in the woodland, a picked blues riff was as yellow as a buttercup, and a rock solo echoed back red and purple, so vivid and strong he had to close his eyes.

His sigil gave him a burst of soft heat, and the guitar thrummed, expectant, as he led into Lizzie's old favorite.

As fair art thou, my bonnie lass,
So deep in love am I,
And I will love thee still, my dear,
Till a' the seas gang dry.

44

The guitar rang, he sang—and suddenly she was there, his Lizzie, her clear high vocal ringing loud and vibrant in a room that was bathed in soft watery blues and greens, as if the ocean lapped at the walls.

Till a' the seas gang dry, my dear,
And the rocks melt wi' the sun,
And I will love thee still, my dear,
While the sands o' life shall run.

The last chord faded and echoed, the valves went dim and cold, and John sat there for long minutes, tears streaming down his face, sadness and joy in equal measure.

It was only after he recovered his composure that he realized the valves had gone dim because the car battery had given out. Otherwise he might still be playing yet, lost long ago and far away in the dance of music and color and memory.

He put the guitar down, reluctantly, for Lizzie was back, and she was the only reason he was here at all.

But there's still a job to be done.

The germ of an idea was forming—he didn't have enough to go on yet, but the performance of the valves had given him something that he had been lacking—hope.

He picked up the leather-bound journal he'd found in the basement, thinking there might be something he could use. The notes were all written in the same neat, perfectly readable hand. Unfortunately it all seemed to be the worst kind of gobbledygook, filled with speculation on the nature of the Outer Darkness, much talk of spheres of influence, and some long rituals in Latin that made no sense to John at all. He was

45

about to close the book when one passage caught his eye—a single word was all it took to get his attention.

"Something snuffled.

"But I would not allow any of us to break the circle, for I well knew just how devious the Outer Realms can be, and I had not yet forgotten the blank stares of the rank of swine creatures in the depths of that black pyramid.

"It was almost morning. Watery sunshine started to leak in through the boards on the windows, its light competing with the glare from the valves, threatening to attenuate what little power was left in the battery. But my companions visibly relaxed; some of the coldness seemed to leech away with the growing light. Doig had even gone as far as starting to light a pipe when there was a loud crash from somewhere below us.

"I knew immediately where the noise had originated—one of the swine things had just tested the strength of the basement door. I remembered the hinges squealing earlier, and in my mind's eye saw them buckle, saw screws fly across the flagstones on the floor, saw a mass of swine things crowding in the doorway to get inside, to get at us.

"I called out the spell—my last hope.

"Ri linn cothrom na meidhe, Ri linn sgathadh na h-anal.

"Ri linn tabhar na breithe Biodh a shith air do theannal fein.

"Dhumna Ort!

"The pounding on the door continued like the sounding of a kettledrum. It reverberated around us

and snook dust from the shelves until finally it stopped. There was one final, almost disappointed, snuffle, then all fell quiet."

John put the notebook down, trying to quell a growing excitement. He had a transcription of the Gaelic spell; an exorcism, the writer called it. He also had the electric pentacle.

Maybe I've found the way to nip this thing in the bud.

But there was still the issue of using another resident's totem—he had no idea how he might use the information he had garnered without causing more problems in the house than he fixed.

He put tape six in the cassette player, hoping to find another clue.

"I have heard her again—the giggle is unmistakable. Just knowing she is near makes what I must do now easier. For even if I fail, I now know there is no ending, I will see her again, somewhere, over her rainbow.

"The old concierge finally, after much persuasion and the offer of some bottles of single malt, agreed to me using the pentacle, one last time. He has taken everyone out to a local pub for a drink—he didn't ask so much as insisted, and I get the feeling the patrons value his opinion above any other when it comes to matters of the house. The result is that I have the place to myself. All is still—perhaps too still, for there is a sense that the house is just waiting for me to make my move, ready with its own countermove.

"Having quiet is good in a way though, as it means that any recording I do should capture all the nuances of what must be done. I have already set up the circle in number seven, and the concierge has lent me a fresh car battery from his shed. All that remains now is for me to switch it on, step inside and start the spell. As before, I shall leave the tape running. Time alone will tell whether this is in fact a good idea."

The tape went quiet—not white noise this time, for John heard the pad of footsteps on carpet, and a distant hum, as if a piece of electrical equipment had just been switched on. Then the man started chanting—Latin this time—a lot of Latin. The sound took on a strange echoing quality, as if recorded in a vast cathedral rather than a small room in a townhouse, and the man sounded as if he were far away, yet loud and close at the same time. Something snuffled, loudly, as if pressed up against the recording microphone, and the man's chanting took on a desperate, almost pleading tone. Latin changed to Gaelic, a cadence that was now becoming strangely familiar, shouted, almost a scream.

"Ri linn cothrom na meidhe, Ri linn sgathadh na h-anal.

"Ri linn tabhar na breithe Biodh a shith air do theannal fein.

"Dhumna Ort!"

Once again everything fell quiet.

The tape ran for several minutes, only a distant electrical hum to tell that anything was being recorded. Then even that was switched off.

"I think it might have worked," the man's voice said softly.

He was immediately answered.

Somewhere, in the far distance, a child giggled.

48

John didn't even get time to rewind the tape before the pounding began again in number seven, even louder and more frantic than before. The door gave way before he made it out of his chair.

When he reached the hallway, the beast was already coming down the stairs. He only got a quick impression of it—low to the floor, a bundle of pinkish fat and muscle and stink. It knocked John aside and barreled through the basement door, almost knocking it off its hinges.

There was a last loud snuffle from somewhere down in the dark, someone upstairs screamed, then the whole house was in an uproar.

—8—

It was close to midnight before John got the house settled into something that resembled normality.

The door to number seven was back in position, although he'd need to get a new one sooner rather than later. Likewise, with Mr. Laws's help, he'd managed to get the basement door back up and locked. That had been a bad half hour, waiting to see if something was going to launch itself out of the darkness below.

There was no sign of Mrs. Gemmell. Her room had been completely trashed, as if something heavy had rampaged through it in fury, and the white sheepskin carpet was smeared with a viscous liquid that looked foul and smelled worse. It was a blessed relief to close the door on the chaos and go back down to his apartment.

He hoped that was the end to the night's surprises, but he found that he couldn't settle. His gaze kept turning to the electric pentacle and his guitar, remembering the brief moment of calm he'd achieved earlier. Then he'd look at the cassette player, and the leather notebook, and remember there was still a job to be done.

Does it have to be right now?

He already knew the answer—old Mr. Laws had given it to him straight, right after they'd fixed the basement door.

"Get this sorted, laddie. Get it sorted tonight, before the house decides it needs a new concierge."

Around one o' clock he gave up pretending. He walked out to his car in the back garage and removed the battery—it wasn't as if he used it much anyway. Then he took it, and all the electric pentacle paraphernalia, down to the basement.

It was time to take his house back from the interloper.

He made a lot of purposeful noise on his way down, if only to make aware to whatever awaited him that he was coming. He stood at the foot of the stairs for several seconds, listening, but the basement was quiet. Maybe too quiet.

He moved quickly to the center of the room, toward the faded outline of the original pentacle. He sketched over the original lines in fresh chalk, and repeated with both holy water and dry garlic—*in for a penny, in for a pound*—then set the valves of the electric pentacle in the points and troughs of the five-pointed star on the floor.

I'm as ready as I'll ever be.

He attached the valves to the battery, and, lifting the notebook from the box, stepped inside the protective circle.

He felt something drag at him immediately. The green valve flared, and thick shadows started to swirl around the circle, spinning in an ever-widening vortex, an inverted cone with John in it, at the bottom. The tugging in his mind grew more insistent. He thought about using the exorcism spell there and then, but there seemed to be no immediate danger, and curiosity got the better of him. He gave in to the tugging, and went with it, and he spun inside the vortex at a dizzying velocity. There was a brilliant flash, then all was velvet blackness.

It took several seconds for his eyes to adjust.

We're not in Kansas anymore, Toto.

He seemed to be approaching a dim red star, spluttering and fizzing in its death throes. Several planets, mere dots traveling across that red surface at first, span around it, and it seemed he had reached his destination. With some renewed haste, he tumbled down toward one of the planets; a rocky globe, its surface studded with craters, punctuated by purple growth that infested the area like patches of moist mold. There was no sign of any seas, nor clouds for that matter.

As he approached the surface he saw, far to the north, a volcano that reached to the sky, sending long plumes of lava spurting into the heavens. He slowed, hovering above a plain under a dark purple sky, with black stems rising, casting shadows from a moon, too large for the sky, a red moon that rose above jagged hills. Things moved among the stems, low-slung and insect-like, farmers tending to the growth.

He started to distinguish landmarks, started to recognize places. With a start he realized that he was looking down over a future landscape—a dim, distant future where the works of man had all but disappeared completely. But some things yet remained, the most prominent of which was a small volcanic knob of rock jutting up from an otherwise flat patch of ground. Lava poured from a crater rim and ran down over walls of broken and tumbled stone. But John knew it far too well not to know the outline—the rock was in Edinburgh, and the crumbled stone was all that was left of the fine castle. As for the city itself, nothing remained. Where once the New Town had been was now a mass of the purple foliage, and the Royal Mile was a snaking river of lava, with no sign of any of the fine townhouses that had once stood there. A glance north showed that Arthur's Seat had survived the ravages of time, rounder and softer than he remembered it, but still distinctive. But of the old coastal towns of Leith and Portobello there was nothing remaining but dust and rock.

And there—squat and low, smack in the middle of where the Grassmarket had once been—the black pyramid sat like a bloated spider. On the eastern side of the black edifice John saw another structure of tumbled rock and stone, a square patch of masonry that he knew intuitively was the remains of the house—his house.

He felt the tugging again, an insistent drag, and felt himself—his consciousness, his very soul—being dragged down toward the pyramid. A cold fear gripped him tight. He knew, he just knew that if he went down there, he wasn't coming back, at least not as anything human. Without even having to read it, he brought the exorcism ritual to mind and called it out, as loud as he could manage.

"*Ri linn cothrom na meidhe, Ri linn sgathadh na h-anal.*

"*Ri linn tabhar na breithe Biodh a shith air do theannal fein.*

"*Dhumna Ort!*"

A thunderclap went off in his brain and everything went black.

When he came to his senses, what was mere seconds later, it seemed, he was lying inside the protective circle, back in the basement of the house. Something stood, just outside the protections, watching him. At first he thought it must be the porcine thing from number seven, but this one was most definitely male. White tusks, as sharp as any razor, caught the dancing auras of light from the valves as it raised a damp snout and snuffled. Below the neck the thing looked superficially like a human, although there were rolls of pink fat in places, and taut sinew and muscle in the shoulders and arms—arms that came to an end not in hands, but in coarse, cloven hooves. The head was squat, almost round, and covered in wiry stubble of coarse hair. Stumpy pointed ears looked too pink, too fleshy. Tiny eyes, like black pearls, were sunk in near shadow above a stubby snout with wide, flaring nostrils, and the evil tusks, a foot long each, curving back on themselves to end in sharp points that looked capable of impaling the strongest flesh. A caustic, stinging stench permeated the air, causing John to gag as he shed tears from his eyes.

He was still struggling to comprehend what he was seeing when the swine thing pawed at the air, as if distracted by the swirling dance of light from the pentacle. And the pentacle itself seemed to react, the blue valve flashing in time to the waving of the thing's arms.

The beast snuffled loudly and stamped its feet. The valves flashed in time.

It raised its head and roared. The red valve pulsed and, as if angered, the swine thing punched at the swirling colors in the air ahead of it. The whole dome of protection in which John stood rang, as if struck like a bell.

The beast roared again, bellowing in rage. It threw itself forward against the swirling aura of the pentacle. The blue, green and yellow valves burst as bright as sunlight, sending the snuffling thing cowering away into a corner, arms raised over its head, only a single black eye peeking through, keeping its gaze fixed on John and the pentacle as it snuffled piteously.

The valves quieted, sending out a wash of pale yellows and soft oranges, like dusk on an autumnal evening. The beast's breathing became less rapid, less heavy. It calmed and went still as the color washed over it. Within minutes the thing was huddled in the corner, sound asleep.

John left the electric pentacle running and stepped carefully over the lines. He had a last look into the corner, making sure the swine thing was not merely shamming and waiting to pounce, then he turned and fled up stairs, three at a time.

It may have stopped its attack, but the beast remained in the cellar.

In the house.

He had failed.

—9—

It wasn't failure he thought about as he poured himself a tall stiffener of Scotch—it was the vision of the black pyramid, sitting in the tumbled ruin of the future city.

He remembered something else the old concierge had told him.

"The house is, the house was, the house always fucking will be. That's just the way it is. There's no use fucking with it."

No use fucking with it? Then how do I fix it?

He replaced the tapes in the cassette player, loading up the seventh, and last. He expected to hear the same cultured tones from all the other recordings, so was surprised when the speaker this time turned out to be the gruff tones of the old concierge—the same man who had introduced John to the house.

> *"Well, he went and fucked with it anyway— and he did something right, I'll give him that. He just didnae understand what he was playing with.*
>
> *"After he got his sigil, I thought he might settle, but even the wee giggling lassie didnae*

stop him—he went up into number seven and did his thing. I think he even got the fucker. At least it's not been back since, but that might just be because they've finished the roadwork outside.

"We offered him a place; it was obvious he belonged, and room five was sitting empty. I think the mannie might even have been happy here. He had his sigil, and this wee box of tricks I'm talking into here turned out to be his totem, although neither he nor I knew it at the time.

"He could have heard his wee lassie anytime he wanted, but he never realized until it was too late. I found him dead down in the basement this morning. He'd been fucking about with that damned pentacle again—he just could nae leave well enough alone.

"You don't fuck with another man's totem— I told him that, and it's his own stupid fault if he didnae listen.

"So now it's finished, thank fuck. I'll take these things down here and lock them away. If anybody is hearing this, then you've found it, you've fucked with it, and you're as stupid as he was at the end.

"Remember—if the shite works, don't fuck with it."

The tape ran out to white noise, but John wasn't listening. It was all a blur in his mind—the ageless nature of the house, sigils and totems, stillness and calm, chaos and noise.

The old guitar rang in sympathy, and the simple chord calmed him immediately.

"It's the bloody tapes themselves," John whispered. "I get it now."

You don't fuck with another man's totem.

The guitar rang again, and his sigil sent him a burst of comforting warmth. The house might be out of balance—but it still knew its job.

And so do I.

He started by taking the cassette player and all the tapes back down to the basement.

The beast was still in the dark corner, snuffling quietly, washed by waves of yellow and soft red, serenaded by a constant soft hum from the pentacle. John placed the recorder and tapes in the center of the circle and the creature did not stir.

Then John did what he realized he should have done some time ago. He went back to his room, fetched the guitar, then took it downstairs. He sat, two steps from the bottom, and started to play.

As fair art thou, my bonnie lass,
So deep in love am I.

Lizzie came in, earlier than usual, closer than ever before, her voice joining his, with the guitar ringing in perfect harmony. The pentacle washed the basement in blues and greens and once again it was as if they sat on an ocean shore with the sun playing on the water and waves lapping at the shore.

And I will love thee still, my dear,
Till a' the seas gang dry.

The beast in the corner slumped into a sitting position. It was hard to see through the swirling dance of color, but it seemed to be fading back into the dark. There might have been a soft, distant snuffle, but John was too far lost in the song, in his love, to take any notice. The guitar rang, he sang—and his Lizzie sat beside him, her clear, high vocal ringing loud and clear as the ocean splashed the walls.

Till a' the seas gang dry, my dear,
And the rocks melt wi' the sun,

The valves were fading again as the battery ran down, but it only took one look into the dark corner to see the job was done—nothing there now but shadow. John kept singing, bringing the song to a close.

And I will love thee still, my dear,
While the sands o' life shall run.

Just as he stopped playing, the tape player in the pentacle started to run.

A child giggled in the far distance.

The lights faded and died, and the last echoing chord from the guitar rang clear and true before silence swallowed the room.

———————

John locked the basement door behind him as he went back up to the house.

High above, someone sobbed, and that quickly turned into a wail of despair—Mrs. Gemmell in number seven. It sounded like she had returned from wherever she had been—and had discovered the mess in her room.

But he could deal with that.

59

His sigil sent him a burst of warmth, the guitar rang loudly as he returned it to his apartment.

John smiled as he continued upstairs to number seven.

It was his job, after all.

About the Author

William Meikle is a Scottish writer, now living in Canada, with over thirty novels published in the genre press and more than 300 short story credits in thirteen countries. He has books available from a variety of publishers including Dark Regions Press and Severed Press and his work has appeared in a large number of professional anthologies and magazines. He lives in Newfoundland with whales, bald eagles and icebergs for company. When he's not writing he drinks beer, plays guitar, and dreams of fortune and glory.

BIBLIOGRAPHY

NOVELS
The Green and The Black / Crossroad Press
The Boathouse / Crossroad Press
Ramskull / Crossroad Press
Songs of Dreaming Gods / Crossroad Press
The Dunfield Terror / Crossroad Press
Fungoid / Crossroad Press
The Hole / Crossroad Press
The Exiled / Crossroad Press
Night of the Wendigo / Crossroad Press
The Ravine / Dark Regions Press
The Invasion / Dark Regions Press
The Valley / Dark Regions Press
The Creeping Kelp / Dark Regions Press
Crustaceans / Dark Regions Press
Sherlock Holmes: The Dreaming Man / Gryphonwood Press
Berserker / Gryphonwood Press
The Midnight Eye Files: The Amulet / Gryphonwood Press
The Midnight Eye Files: The Sirens / Gryphonwood Press

The Midnight Eye Files: The Skin Game / Gryphonwood Press
The Concordances of the Red Serpent / Gryphonwood Press
Watchers: The Coming of the King / Gryphonwood Press
Watchers: The Battle for the Throne / Gryphonwood Press
Watchers: Culloden / Gryphonwood Press
Watchers: Omnibus edition / Gryphonwood Press
Eldren: The Book of the Dark / Gryphonwood Press
Island Life / Gryphonwood Press
The Road Hole Bunker Mystery - Charade Media

NOVELLAS

Operation: North Pole / Severed Press
Operation: Orkney / Severed Press
Operation: Patagonia / Severed Press
Operation: London / Severed Press
Operation: Sahara / Severed Press
Operation: Yukon / Severed Press
Operation: North Sea / Severed Press
Operation: Congo / Severed Press
Operation: Mongolia / Severed Press
Operation: Norway / Severed Press
Operation: Syria / Severed Press
Operation: Loch Ness / Severed Press
Operation: Amazon / Severed Press
Operation: Siberia/ Severed Press
Operation: Antarctica / Severed Press
Infestation / Severed Press
The Lost Valley / Severed Press
Sea Hunters: Shonisaurus / Severed Press
The Land Below / Severed Press
The Sea Below / Severed Press
The City Below / Severed Press
Tormentor / Crossroad Press

Clockwork Dolls / Crossroad Press
Sigils and Totems: A Collection of Novellas / Crossroad Press
Broken Sigil / Crossroad Press
Pentacle / Crossroad Press
The Job / Crossroad Press
The House on the Moor / Dark Regions Press
The Plasm / Dark Regions Press
Professor Challenger: The Island of Terror / Dark Regions Press
Sherlock Holmes: Revenant / Dark Regions Press

SHORT STORY COLLECTIONS
Inspector Lestrade: The Black Temple / Weird House Press
The Ghost Club / Crystal Lake Publishing
Dark Melodies / Dark Regions Press
Carnacki: Heaven and Hell / Dark Regions Press
Carnacki: The Watcher at the Gate / Dark Regions Press
Carnacki: The Edinburgh Townhouse / Lovecraft ezine
Carnacki: Starry Wisdom / Dark Regions Press
Sherlock Holmes: The Quality of Mercy / Dark Regions Press
Professor Challenger: The Kew Growths / Dark Regions Press
The Midnight Eye Files: Omnibus / Gryphonwood Press
The Midnight Eye Files: Omnibus 2 / Gryphonwood Press
Samurai and Other Stories / Crystal Lake Publishing
Myth and Monsters / KnightWatch Press

Curious about other Crossroad Press books? Stop by our
website: http://crossroadpress.com
We offer quality writing
in digital, audio, and print formats.

Subscribe to our newsletter on the website homepage and
receive a free eBook.